THE TIES THAT BIND

A STORY OF LOVE, BETRAYAL, AND REDEMPTION

RAGINI DEVI

To my family, for their unwavering love and support in the creation of this book. The ties that bind us together are unbreakable, and it is through them that I am able to tell this story. Thank you for always being there for me, through every chapter of my life.

To all those who have ever felt tied down, by the weight of their past or the expectations of others, this book is for you. May it remind you that you have the strength and resilience to break free and chase your dreams. And to those who have been a source of love and encouragement, thank you for being the ties that have held me together.

And finally, to my readers, thank you for taking the time to dive into the world of this book. It is through your support and engagement that these stories come to life and continue to be shared. I hope that the characters and their struggles will resonate with you and remind you that you are not alone in your journey. The ties that bind us together can also be the ties that set us free

Contents

Foreword

The ties that bind us can be both a source of strength and a source of struggle. They are the connections we have to our family, our friends, and our past. They shape who we are and who we become. In this book, Ragini Devi expertly explores these ties, delving into the complexities of relationships and the weight of our pasts.

Through the eyes of the characters, we see the power of love, the pain of loss, and the resilience of the human spirit. We are taken on a journey of self-discovery, as the characters learn to navigate the ties that bind them and the ties they must break. Ragini Devi has crafted a story that is both poignant and relatable, one that will resonate with readers of all ages and backgrounds.

It is a testament to the power of storytelling and the impact that literature can have on our lives. I urge you to take the time to read this book, to immerse yourself in the world of the characters and to reflect on the ties that bind you. I have no doubt that you will come away from this book with a newfound appreciation for the power of our connections and the strength we can find within ourselves.

Preface

The ties that bind us can be both a source of strength and a source of struggle. They are the connections we have to our family, our friends, and our past. They shape who we are and who we become. In this book, [Author's Name] expertly explores these ties, delving into the complexities of relationships and the weight of our pasts.

Through the eyes of the characters, we see the power of love, the pain of loss, and the resilience of the human spirit. We are taken on a journey of self-discovery, as the characters learn to navigate the ties that bind them and the ties they must break. [Author's Name] has crafted a story that is both poignant and relatable, one that will resonate with readers of all ages and backgrounds.

It is a testament to the power of storytelling and the impact that literature can have on our lives. I urge you to take the time to read this book, to immerse yourself in the world of the characters and to reflect on the ties that bind you. I have no doubt that you will come away from this book with a newfound appreciation for the power of our connections and the strength we can find within ourselves."

write preface of the book

"When I began writing this book, I had no idea the journey it would take me on. The characters and their stories quickly took on a life of their own, leading me down paths I never could have predicted. As I wrote, I found myself reflecting on my own experiences and the ties that have shaped my life.

The theme of this book, "The ties that bind," is one that I believe is universal. We all have connections to our past and to the people in our lives that shape who we are. These ties can be a source of strength, but they can also be a source of struggle. I wanted to explore this concept in a way that was both relatable and thought-provoking.

Through the eyes of the characters, we see the power of love, the pain of loss, and the resilience of the human spirit. We are taken on a journey of self-discovery, as the characters learn to navigate the ties that bind them and the ties they must break. I hope that this book will resonate with readers of all ages and backgrounds, and that it will serve as a reminder that we all have the strength and resilience to break free and chase our dreams.

I hope that you will take the time to read this book, to immerse yourself in the world of the characters, and to reflect on the ties that bind you.

Acknowledgements

Writing this book has been a journey, and I am so grateful for the support and encouragement I have received along the way.

First and foremost, I would like to thank my family for their unwavering love and support. They have been my rock through every chapter of this process and I couldn't have done it without them.

I also want to extend my gratitude to my beta readers, who provided valuable feedback and helped me to see the story from different perspectives. Their insights were invaluable in shaping the final product.

I would like to thank my agent and editor, who believed in this book from the start and guided me through the publishing process. Their enthusiasm and guidance was instrumental in bringing this book to fruition.

And finally, I want to thank my readers. Without your support, this book would not be possible. Thank you for taking the time to read my words and for allowing me to share my story with you.

Prologue

The ties that bind us are not always visible. They are the threads that connect us to our past, to our family, to our friends, and to ourselves. They shape who we are and who we become, but they can also hold us back.

For Mary, the ties that bind her are the memories of her past, the expectations of her family, and the weight of her own regrets. Growing up in a small town, she had always dreamed of something more, but she never imagined the sacrifices she would have to make to chase her dreams.

For John, the ties that bind him are the secrets of his past, the memories of his father, and the fear of not living up to his expectations. He is held captive by the guilt of his past and the fear of his future.

For Sally, the ties that bind her are the memories of her mother, the guilt of her past, and the fear of never being able to move on. She is trapped in the past and struggles to find her way forward.

This is a story of the ties that bind us and the ties we must break to be free. It's a story of love, loss, and resilience, as the characters learn to navigate the ties that bind them and the ties they must break. It's a story that will make you question your own ties and question what you would do to break them.

CHAPTER ONE

The ties that bind us

Once upon a time, in a far-off land, there lived a young prince named Alexander. He was handsome and strong, but also proud and selfish. He spent his days hunting and feasting with his companions, never thinking of the needs of his people.

One day, while on a hunting trip, Alexander became lost in the forest. As night fell, he stumbled upon a small cottage in the clearing. Inside, he found an old woman who offered to take him in for the night.

The old woman was kind and hospitable, and Alexander soon found himself telling her of his exploits and his desire for power. The old woman listened patiently, but when he had finished, she said, "My dear prince, you have everything a man could want, but you are missing the most important thing of all: love. Without love, all your wealth and power will mean nothing."

Alexander was taken aback by her words, but as he lay in bed that night, he couldn't shake the feeling that she was right. He realized that he had been so focused on himself that he had neglected the people he was meant to serve and protect.

The next morning, Alexander thanked the old woman for her wisdom and set out to return home. As he journeyed back, he began to think about the ties that bind us all together - the ties of family, friendship, and community. He realized that true happiness and fulfillment could only be found by serving others and building strong relationships.

When he returned home, Alexander began to make changes. He visited the sick and the poor, and he worked to improve the lives of his people. He also made amends with his friends and family, who had grown distant during his time of selfishness.

Years passed, and Alexander's kingdom prospered. He had become a wise and just ruler, beloved by all. And when he passed away, his people mourned the loss of their king, but also celebrated his life and the love he had shared with them.

The moral of the story: "The ties that bind us" are the most important things in life, more than wealth and power. True happiness and fulfillment can only be found by serving others and building strong relationships.

CHAPTER TWO

Breaking free

Once upon a time, in a small village, there lived a young girl named Sarah. She was smart and ambitious, but her life was controlled by her strict and domineering father. He dictated what she should wear, who she should talk to, and even what she should study. Sarah felt trapped and suffocated by her father's control.

One day, Sarah met a kind and understanding teacher who saw her potential and encouraged her to pursue her dreams. With her teacher's support, Sarah began to break free from her father's hold and make her own choices. She started taking classes in subjects that she was passionate about, and she even made friends outside of her strict social circle.

As Sarah's confidence grew, she began to challenge her father's authority. She spoke up for herself and refused to be controlled by his rules. At first, her father was furious and tried to punish her for her defiance. But Sarah stood firm and eventually, her father began to see that she was capable of making her own decisions.

It was not easy, and there were many conflicts and struggles. But Sarah realized that she had to break free from her father's control to find true happiness and fulfillment. And in the end, her father realized that he was holding her back and let her go.

Years passed, and Sarah went on to achieve great success in her field, and she lived a happy and fulfilling life. She never forgot the lessons she learned about breaking free from the control of others and following her own path.

The moral of the story: Breaking free from the control of others can be difficult, but it is necessary to find true happiness and fulfillment in life. It's important to have the courage to make our own choices and live the life we want.

CHAPTER THREE

The weight of the past

Once upon a time, in a quaint little town, there lived a young man named Jack. He was a hard-working and honest person, but he was haunted by the mistakes of his past. He had made some poor choices and had hurt those he cared about. He carried the weight of his past with him everywhere he went, and it weighed heavily on his mind.

One day, Jack met an old wise man who lived on the outskirts of town. The old man saw the pain in Jack's eyes and offered to help him. The old man told Jack that the past is like a heavy backpack that you carry on your journey through life. It can weigh you down and make it difficult to move forward. But the old man also said that the past is not who you are, it's just something that you have to carry.

With the old man's guidance, Jack began to let go of the past. He apologized to those he had hurt, and he made amends for his mistakes. He realized that he could not change the past, but he could learn from it and use it to make better choices in the future.

Jack also started to focus on the present, and he found joy in the simple things in life. He volunteered in his community, and he started a small business that helped others. He began to feel a sense of purpose and meaning in his life.

Years passed, and Jack became a respected and admired member of the community. He had finally let go of the weight of his past and was able to move forward and live a happy and fulfilling life.

The moral of the story: The weight of the past can hold us back and make it difficult to move forward, but it's essential to learn from our mistakes and let go of it. By focusing on the present, and helping others, we can find purpose and meaning in our lives.

CHAPTER FOUR

The expectations of others

Once upon a time, in a bustling city, there lived a young artist named Ava. She was incredibly talented and passionate about her craft, but she struggled to find her place in the world. She felt pressured by the expectations of others - her parents wanted her to become a lawyer, her friends wanted her to fit in and conform, and the art community expected her to follow the latest trends and styles.

Feeling lost and unsure of herself, Ava stopped painting altogether. She started to feel like a failure and like she would never be good enough to meet the expectations of others. But one day, while wandering through the city, she stumbled upon an old abandoned art studio. Inside, she found a beautiful painting that spoke to her soul. It was a reminder of why she fell in love with art in the first place.

With renewed inspiration and determination, Ava started painting again, this time for herself, not for the expectations of others. She explored different styles and techniques, and she found a unique voice in her work. Her paintings began to catch the attention of the art community, and she gained a following of people who appreciated her art for what it was.

Ava's parents and friends were initially surprised and confused by her new direction, but as they saw the passion and joy that her art brought her, they began to support her fully.

Years passed, and Ava became a successful artist, renowned for her unique style and vision. She realized that the expectations of others should never dictate her choices in life, and that true happiness and fulfillment can only be found by following one's own passion.

The moral of the story: The expectations of others can be overwhelming and can make us lose sight of our own passions and goals. It's important to stay true to ourselves and follow our own path, even if it's different from what others expect of us. By doing so, we can find true happiness and fulfillment in life.

CHAPTER FIVE

The power of love

Once upon a time, in a picturesque kingdom, there lived a young king named Max. He was a just and fair ruler, but he was also cold and distant, believing that love and emotions were weaknesses. He ruled with an iron fist, and his subjects lived in fear of him.

One day, while out on a hunting trip, Max stumbled upon a beautiful and kind-hearted village girl named Emily. She showed him kindness and compassion, despite his cold demeanor. As they spent more time together, Max found himself falling deeply in love with her.

Emily, however, was not impressed by Max's title or wealth, she only saw the cold and distant man he had become. She taught him that love and emotions were not weaknesses, but strengths that could bring people together and make the world a better place.

With Emily's guidance and love, Max began to change. He started to show compassion and empathy to his subjects and worked to improve their lives. He also made peace with his enemies and fostered good relations with neighboring kingdoms.

Max's kingdom began to flourish under his new leadership, and his people loved and respected him. He realized that love was the most powerful force in the world, and that it could bring about change and unity.

Years passed, and Max and Emily got married and had children

, and they ruled the kingdom together as a fair and just team. They were known for their love and compassion towards their people and their kingdom was known as the land of peace and prosperity.

Max's rule was a stark contrast to the way he had ruled before, when he was cold and distant. He realized that without love and compassion, a ruler is nothing but a tyrant.

As time went by, Max and Emily grew old together and passed on the kingdom to their children. The kingdom continued to thrive and the people continued to remember Max and Emily's reign as a golden age, where love and compassion were the guiding principles.

The moral of the story: Love is the most powerful force in the world, it can change people, bring unity and peace, and make the world a better place. Love and compassion should always be at the forefront of leadership. Without love, a ruler is nothing but a tyrant.

CHAPTER SIX

The pain of loss

Once upon a time, there was a young boy named Timmy who lived in a small village nestled in the mountains. He was an adventurous boy, who loved to explore the forests and the streams with his dog, Rusty. Timmy and Rusty were inseparable, and they had many adventures together.

One day, while Timmy and Rusty were exploring the forest, Rusty got lost. Timmy searched everywhere for him, but he couldn't find him. He was devastated and felt like a part of him was missing. He couldn't bear the thought of living without Rusty by his side.

The days passed, and Timmy became increasingly withdrawn and sad. He stopped exploring the forest and stopped playing with his friends. He spent most of his time sitting by the stream where he and Rusty used to play, hoping that Rusty would come back to him.

One day, an old wise man came to Timmy and saw the pain in his eyes. The old man told Timmy that the pain of loss is a natural part of life, but that it's essential to learn from it and move forward. He explained that holding on to the pain of loss will only make it harder to heal, and that it's important to remember the good times and the memories shared with the ones we love.

Timmy took the old man's words to heart and slowly started to heal. He remembered the adventures he had with Rusty and all the good times they shared. He started to explore the forest again, and he found new friends and new adventures. He realized that life goes on and that it's important to cherish the memories of the past and to make new memories for the future.

Years passed, and Timmy grew up to be a wise and adventurous man, always remembering the lessons he learned from his beloved Rusty and the old wise man. He realized that the pain of loss is a part of life, but that it's essential to move forward, to make new memories, and to cherish the memories of the past.

The moral of the story: The pain of loss is a natural part of life, but it's essential to learn from it and move forward. Holding on to the pain of loss will only make it harder to heal, but by remembering the good times and the memories shared with the ones we love, we can find the strength to heal and move forward. It's important to cherish the memories of the past and to make new memories for the future. Life goes on and we must learn to adapt and grow, even in the face of loss. Remembering the love and joy shared with those we've lost, we can continue to live and love fully.

CHAPTER SEVEN

The resilience of the human spirit

Once upon a time, in a small town on the coast, there lived a young woman named Sarah. She was a hardworking and determined person, but she had been dealt a tough hand in life. She grew up in poverty and had to face many challenges, but through it all, she never lost her spirit or her determination.

One day, a terrible storm hit the town and destroyed much of the community, including Sarah's home and her small business. She lost everything she had worked so hard for and was left with nothing but the clothes on her back.

But Sarah didn't give up. She knew that she had the strength and resilience to rebuild and start again. She rallied the community together and they worked tirelessly to clean up the debris and rebuild their homes and businesses.

Despite the setbacks and difficulties, Sarah never lost hope. She knew that the human spirit is incredibly resilient and that with hard work and determination, anything is possible. With the help of her community, Sarah was able to rebuild her home and her business, and she even opened a community center to help others in need.

Years passed, and Sarah's small town thrived again. It was a shining example of the resilience of the human spirit. Sarah's determination and hard work had inspired others to never give up and to keep pushing forward, no matter how tough life got.

Sarah's story of resilience and determination spread far and wide, and she became an inspiration to many people who had faced similar struggles. She proved that no matter how hard life gets, the human spirit has the strength to overcome and rebuild.

But Sarah never forgot the struggles she faced and the hardship of the storm. She knew that not everyone had the same strength and resilience that she did and that it was important to support and help others who are going through difficult times.

In the end, Sarah's story was not just about her own resilience, but about the power of a community coming together to support one another. Her determination to never give up had brought her community together, and they had built something much greater than any of them could have done alone.

The moral of the story: The human spirit is incredibly resilient, and with hard work and determination, anything is possible. Even in the face of hardship and loss, we have the strength to rebuild and move forward. And when a community comes together to support one another, we can achieve great things.

CHAPTER EIGHT

Navigating the ties that bind

Once upon a time, there was a young woman named Grace. She grew up in a tight-knit community where everyone knew each other and looked out for one another. But as she grew older, Grace began to feel suffocated by the constant expectations and obligations placed upon her by her community.

She longed to break free and explore the world outside of her small town. She wanted to see new places and meet new people, but she felt like she couldn't leave her community behind. She felt guilty for wanting to leave, and she didn't want to disappoint her family and friends.

But one day, Grace met a traveler who had seen the world and had many stories to tell. The traveler told her that it's important to follow her dreams and not let the ties that bind her hold her back. The traveler's words resonated with Grace, and she knew that she had to find a way to navigate the ties that bound her.

Grace began to talk to her family and friends about her dreams and her desire to explore the world. They were initially shocked and hurt, but they soon realized that they wanted her to be happy and to follow her dreams. With their support, Grace was able to break free and set out on her journey.

She traveled to many different countries and had many adventures. She met new people and learned new things. She realized that the world was much bigger than she ever imagined, and that there were many different ways to live and many different paths to take.

When she returned home, she was a changed person. She had gained a new perspective on life and had learned the importance of following her dreams. She had also learned how to navigate the ties that bind her and how to balance her desire for freedom with her obligations to her family and community.

The moral of the story: It's important to navigate the ties that bind us, and to find a balance between our desire for freedom and our obligations to our family and community. We should follow our dreams, but we should also be mindful of the people and places that are important to us. It's possible to maintain strong connections with our loved ones while also pursuing our own goals and passions.

Grace's journey taught her that there is no one right way to live and that it's important to listen to your own heart and to make choices that are true to yourself. She realized that while the ties that bind us can be restrictive, they can also be a source of love, support, and strength.

In the end, Grace learned that by communicating openly and honestly with her loved ones and by being true to herself, she was able to navigate the ties that bound her and find a path that was fulfilling and meaningful for her. She returned home with a newfound appreciation for her family and community, and a greater understanding of the importance of balance in life.

CHAPTER NINE

The ties that set us free

Once upon a time, there was a young man named Jack. He was born into a wealthy and influential family, but he felt trapped by the expectations and obligations that came with his privileged upbringing. He longed to break free and find his own path in life, but he felt like he couldn't leave his family behind.

He tried to ignore his feelings and fulfill his familial duties, but he could never shake the feeling that he was living someone else's life. He was always searching for something more.

One day, Jack met a wise old man who told him that the ties that bind us can also set us free. The old man explained that the ties that bind us are not always negative and that they can be a source of love and support. He said that sometimes the ties that bind us are the very things that give us the strength to break free and chase our dreams.

Jack was skeptical, but he decided to give it a try. He began to talk to his family about his feelings and his desire to break free. To his surprise, they were understanding and supportive. They loved him and wanted him to be happy, and they knew that he had a unique talent and passion for photography.

With the support of his family, Jack set out to pursue his dream of becoming a professional photographer. He traveled to different places, capturing the beauty of the world through his lens. He was finally living the life he had always dreamed of.

But as he traveled, he realized that the ties that bound him were not a hindrance but a source of strength. He felt a deep connection to his family and his past, and he knew that they were always with him, cheering him on and supporting him.

The moral of the story: The ties that bind us can also set us free. It's important to be true to ourselves and to follow our dreams, but it's also important to remember the people and places that are important to us. Our family and loved ones can be a source of love and support, and it's important to communicate openly and honestly with them. With their support, we can break free and chase our dreams.

CHAPTER TEN

The journey of self-discovery

Once upon a time, there was a young woman named Emily. She had always felt like something was missing in her life, but she didn't know what it was. She felt unfulfilled in her job and her relationships, and she didn't know what her purpose in life was.

One day, Emily decided to take a trip alone to a remote mountain village. She wanted to clear her head and figure out what was missing in her life. As she hiked through the mountains, she realized that she had been so focused on pleasing others that she had lost touch with herself.

She met a wise old woman in the village who taught her about the importance of self-discovery. The old woman told her that true happiness comes from finding one's own path and living a life that is true to oneself.

Emily took this advice to heart and began to explore the village and its surroundings. She met new people and learned new things. She realized that she had a passion for photography, and she began to take pictures of the breathtaking landscapes around her.

As she explored, she also began to understand that the past experiences and people who had shaped her had an impact on her, and that self-discovery also involved understanding oneself.

As Emily's journey continued, she started to find her own voice and to understand what truly made her happy. She realized that she didn't want to go back to her old life and that she wanted to pursue photography as a career.

The moral of the story: The journey of self-discovery is an ongoing process. It's important to take time to explore and understand ourselves, and to find our own path in life. By being true to ourselves and living a life that is authentic, we can find true happiness and fulfillment. And to achieve that, it's also important to understand oneself, learn from past experiences and people who shape us, and to not be afraid of change.